WHO BROKE THE TEAPOT?!

For Abigail and Molly

Tundra Books, a division of Random House of Canada Limited, a Penguin Random House Company

Library and Archives Canada Cataloguing in Publication

Slavin, Bill, author, illustrator
Who broke the teapot? / Bill Slavin.
Issued in print and electronic formats.
ISBN 978-1-77049-833-4 (bound).—ISBN 978-1-77049-834-1 (epub)
I. Title.
PS8587.L43W46 2016 jC813'.54 C2015-904010-8
C2015-904011-6

Published simultaneously in the United States of America by Tundra Books of Northern New York, a division of Random House of Canada Limited, a Penguin Random House Company

Library of Congress Control Number: 2015947655

Edited by Samantha Swenson
Designed by Bill Slavin
The artwork in this book was rendered in acrylic on gessoed board.
Printed and bound in China

www.penguinrandomhouse.ca

1 2 3 4 5 6 20 19 18 17 16 15

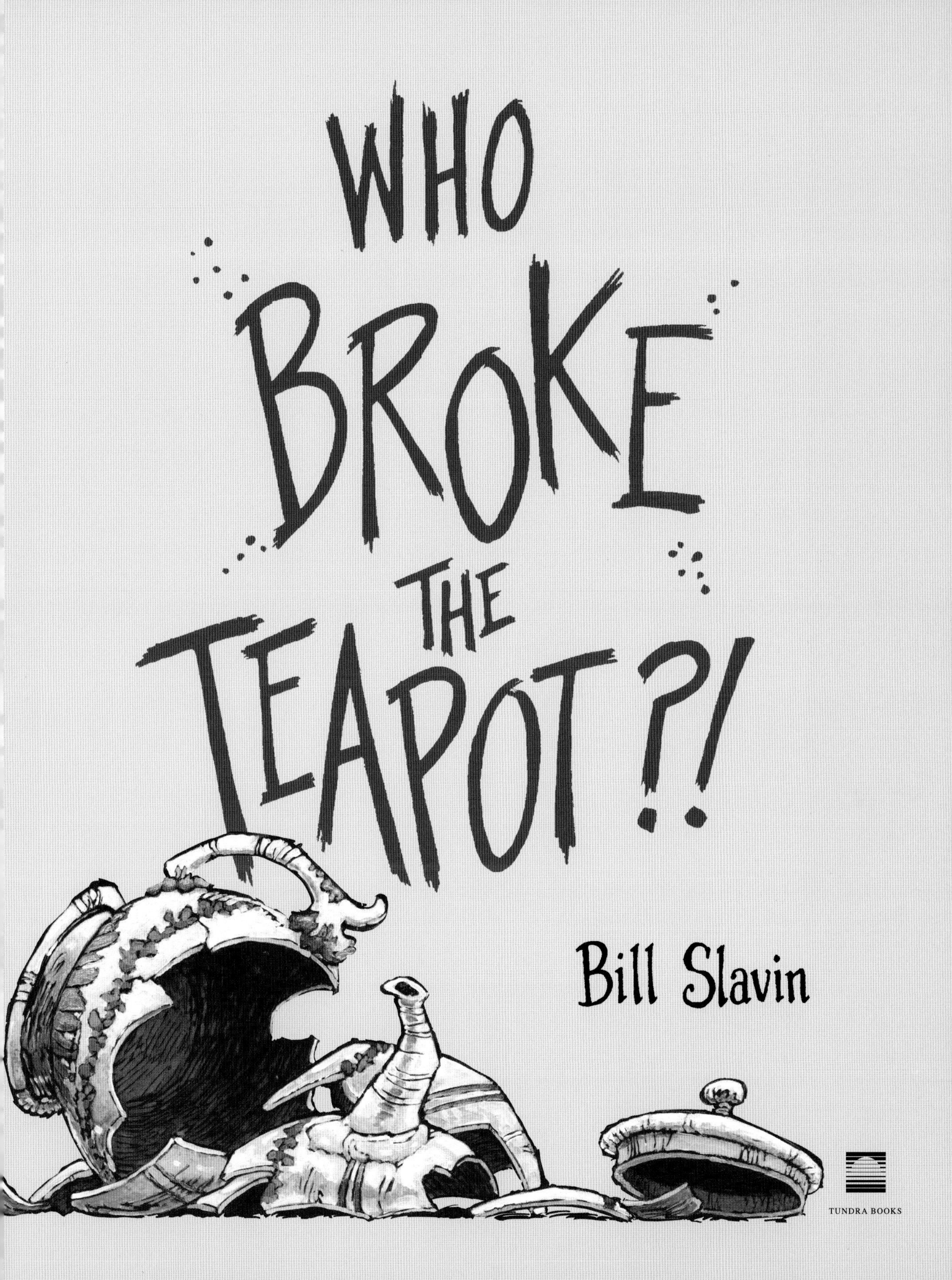
WHO BROKE THE TEAPOT?!
Bill Slavin
TUNDRA BOOKS

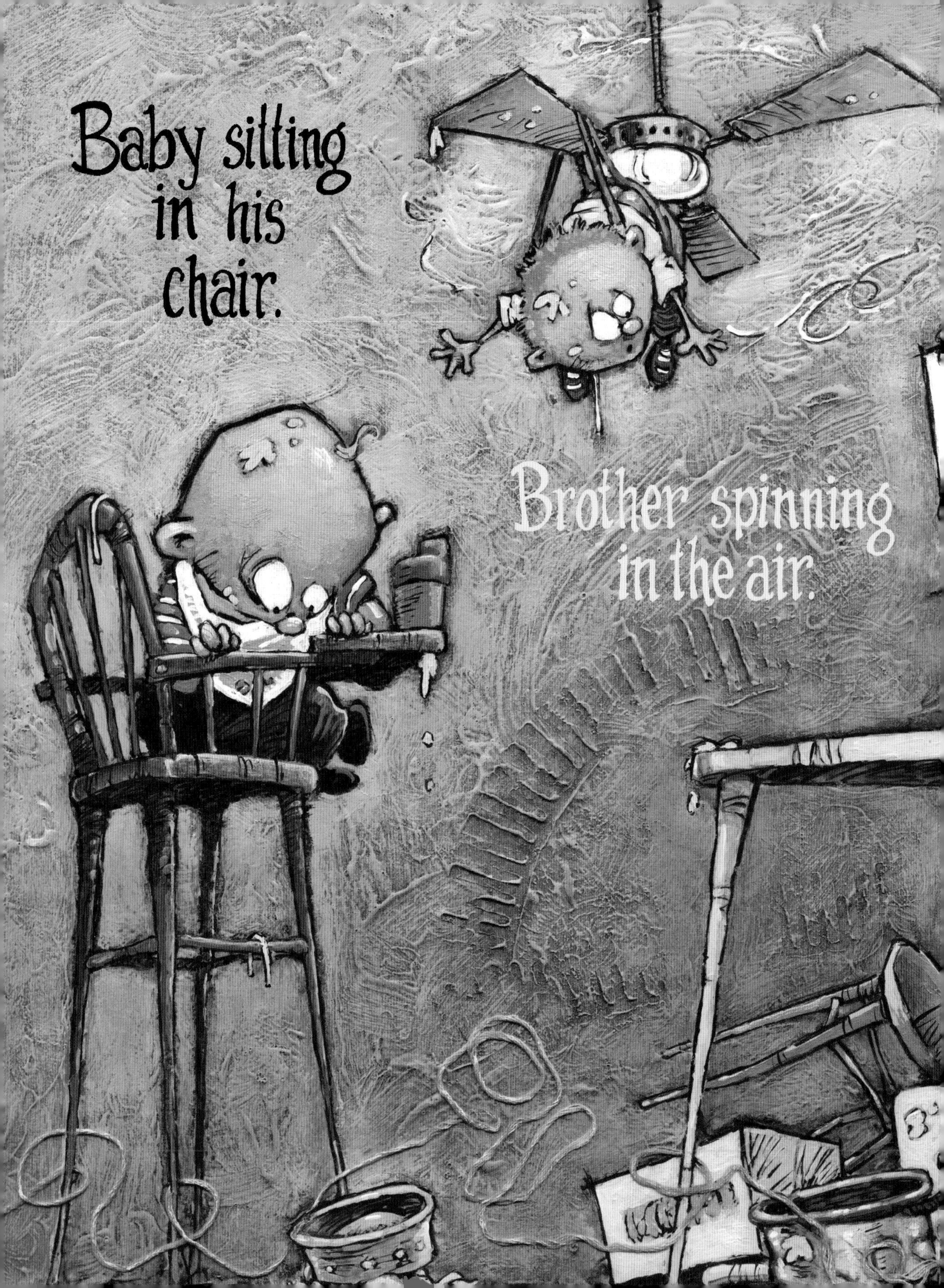
Baby sitting
in his
chair.
Brother spinning
in the air.

PAPA STILL IN UNDERWEAR!
Any complaints?
News Flashes—
Hertogenbosch neutralized
WHO BROKE THE TEAPOT?!

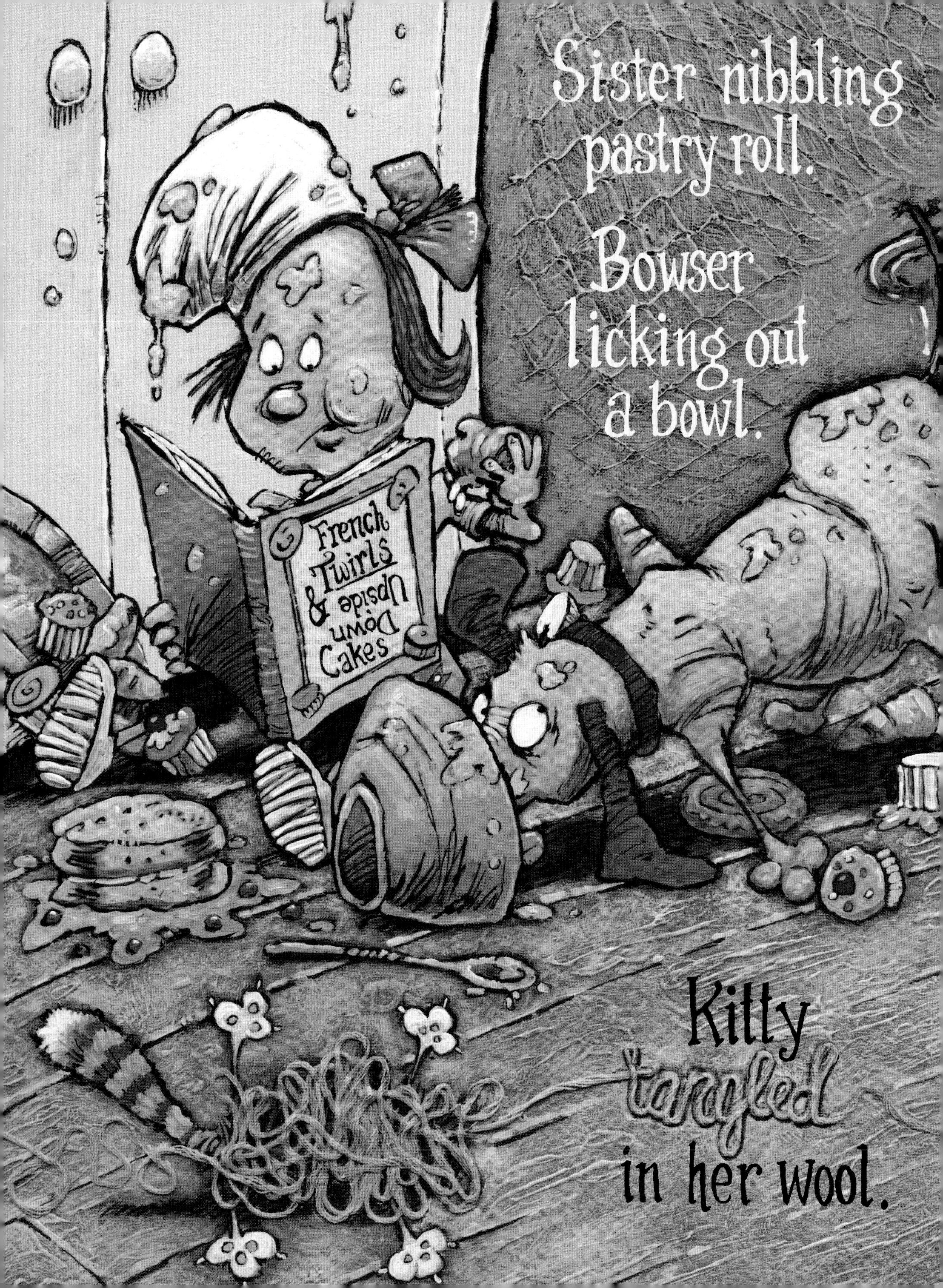
Sister nibbling pastry roll.
Bowser licking out a bowl.
French Twirls & Upside Down Cakes
Kitty tangled in her wool.

Who
Broke
the
TEAPOt
?!

THIS WAS MY VERY BEST TEAPOT!
IT WAS MY FAVORITE OF THE LOT!
IT poured
AND DID NOT SPILL
And kep
the tea sc
nice and ho
A DROP.

I used it for my Ladies Lunch, special days and Sunday Brunch~
AND NOW IT'S LYING HERE ALL CRUNCHED!

WHO BROK
TEAP

THE T?!

"Nog I," says sister,
mouth too full.
"Nor me," barked
Bowser from
his bowl.

Says Kitty,
"Goodness! Bless
my soul! I'm all
tied up inside
this wool!"

Says brother,
spinning in the air,
"If I'm up here
I wasn't there."
"Not my fault!" claims
News Chronicle Crossword

Says Papa, sitting
in his chair,
"I'm only wearing
underwear!
Reading here without
a care!
It was not me.
I swear! I swear!"
Well,
then...

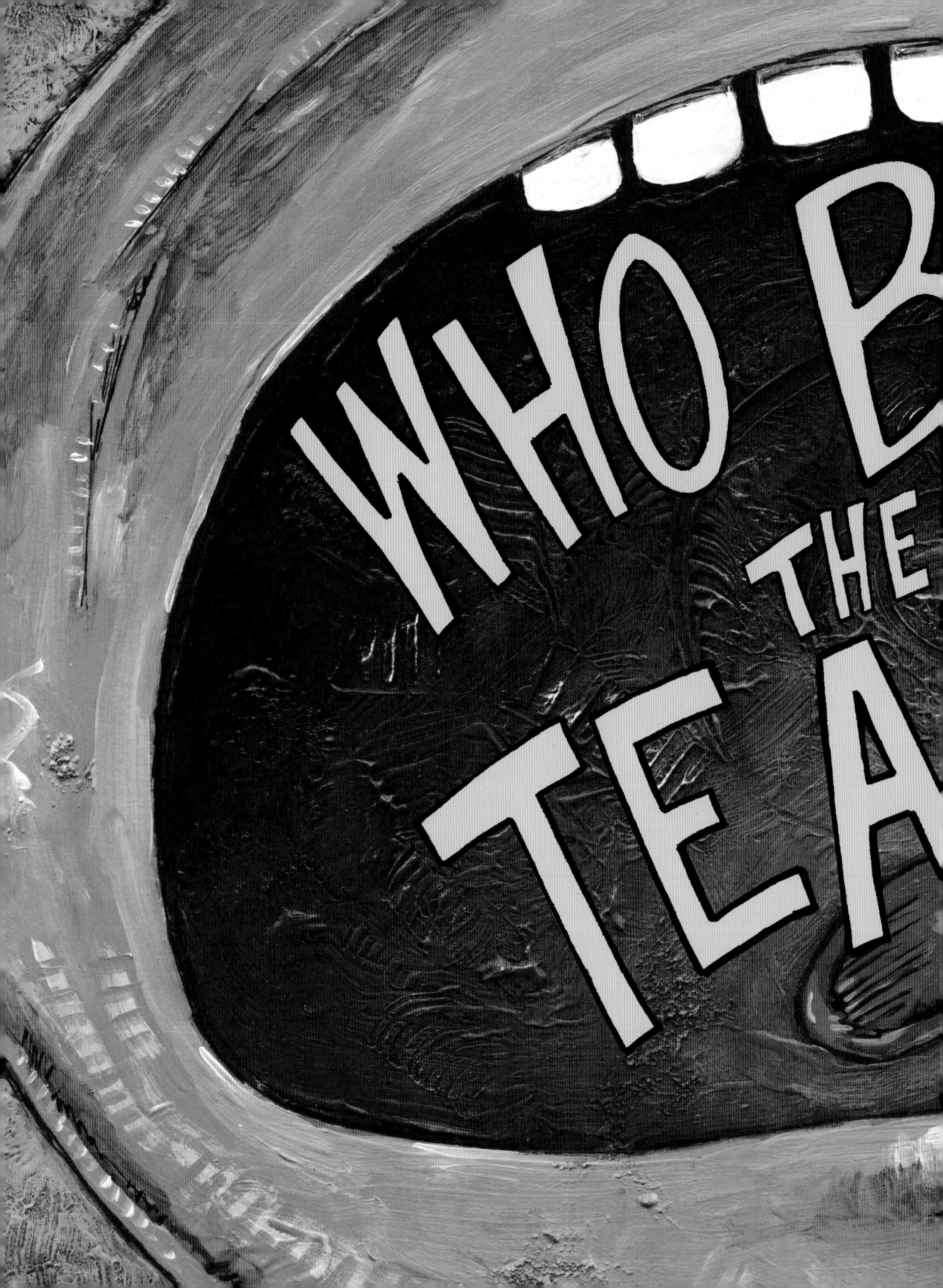

WHO B
THE
TEA

ROKE
OOT?!

BABADOO!
I doubt it.

ALTHOUGH I KNOW TEAPOTS CAN'T FLY...

I ALSO KNOW YOU WOULDN'T LIE. THE TEAPOT'S BROKEN, GONE FOR GOOD.

I would undo it if I could.

BIG SIGH!

BUT STILL I WONDER, AFTER ALL.

WHAT COULD HAVE CAUSED THAT POT TO FALL.

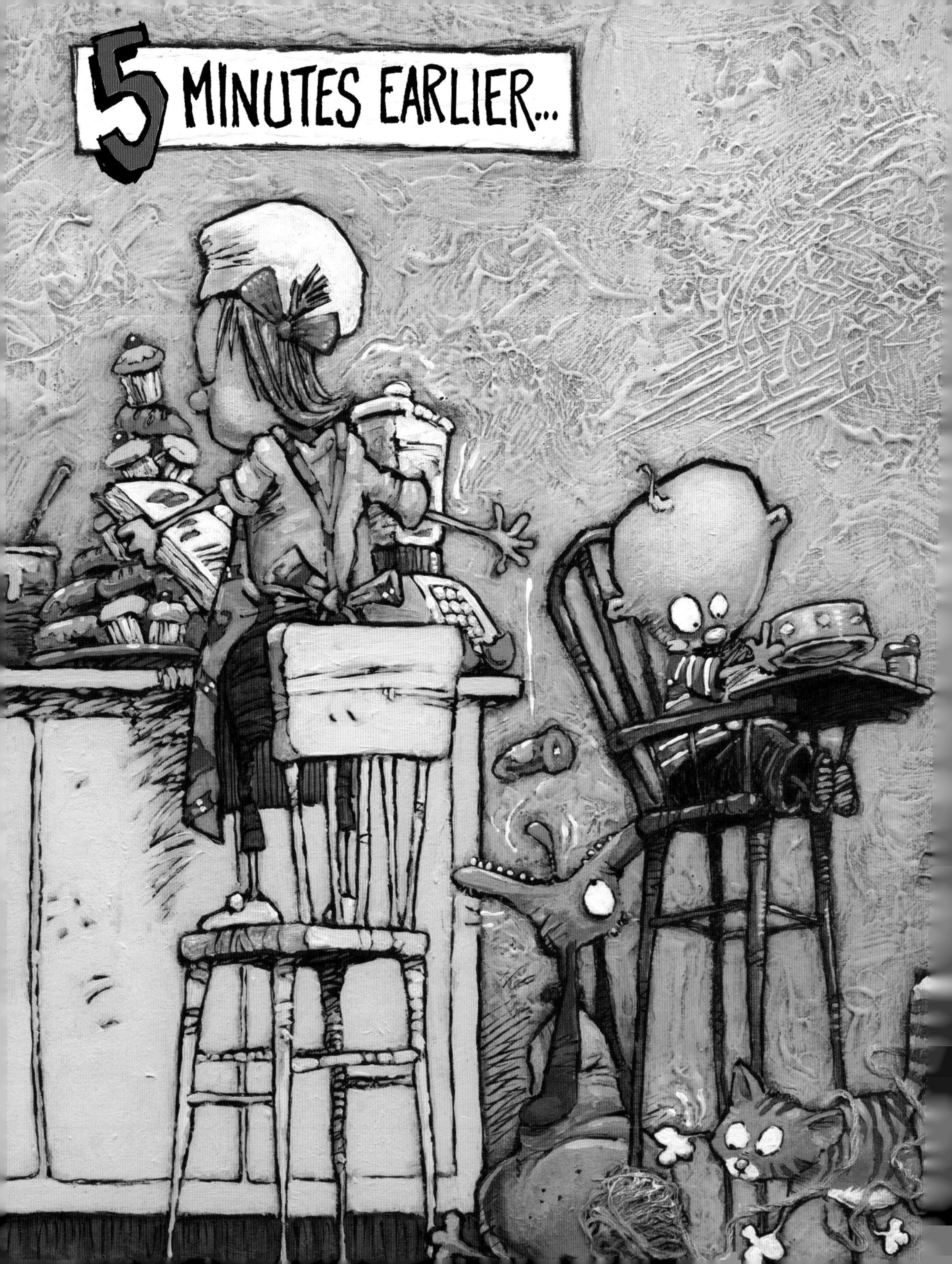
5 MINUTES EARLIER...

Disaster looms warns scientists
Getting hands wet to keep an eye on quality

THUMP!
YOWL!
ROWF! ROWF!

AAARGH!!
SPLAT!
WHIRR!
CLATTER

STOMP!

WHAT IS ALL THAT NOISE??
QUIIIIIIET!!!
STOMP!
STOMP!

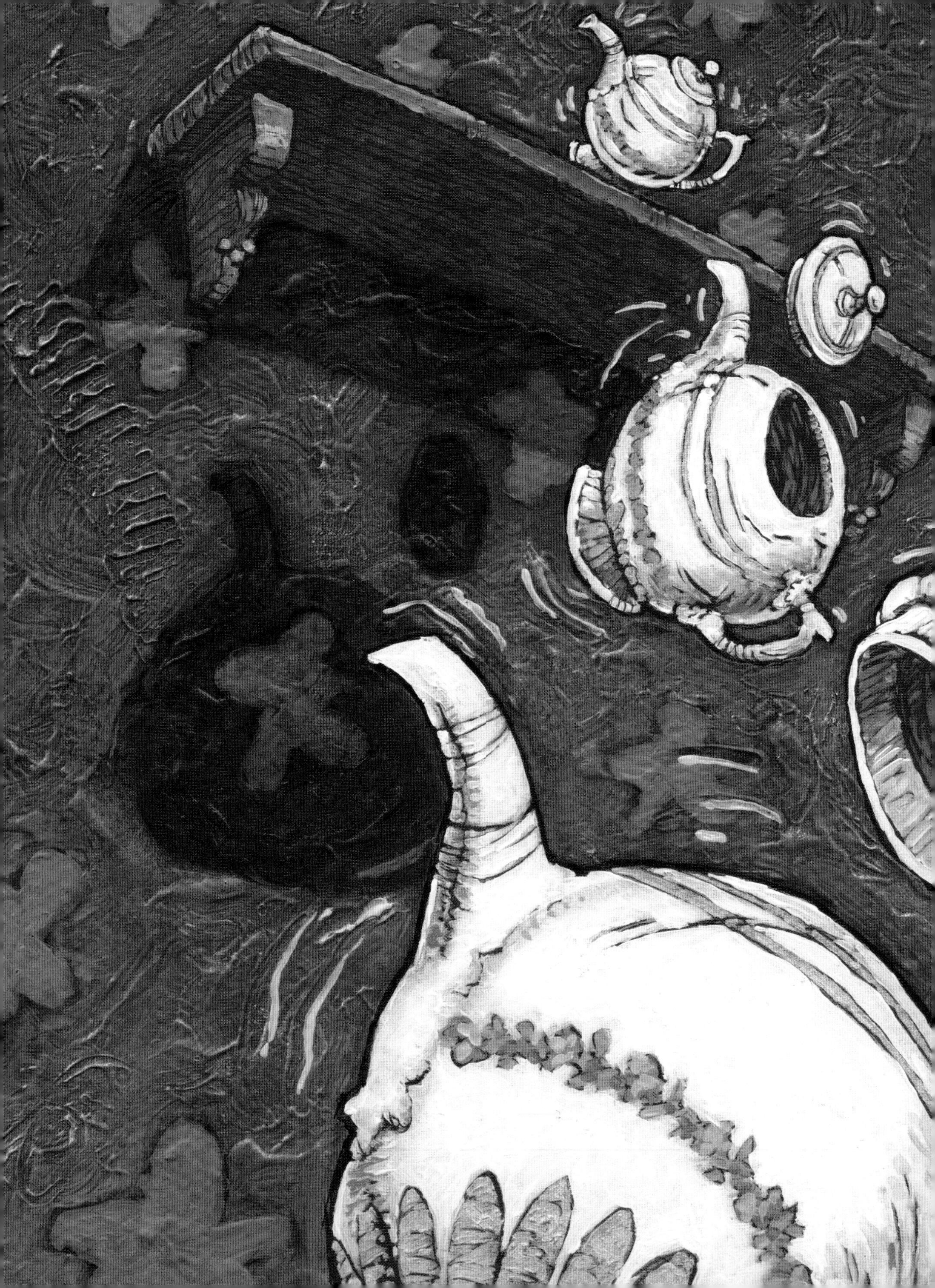

CRASH!!

Tea
tery solved?

So...
who broke
the
teapot?